MW00478317

LOVE

from

Dr. Seuss

Love from Dr. Seuss
TM & © by Dr. Seuss Enterprises, L.P. 2019
All rights reserved

A CIP catalogue record for this title is available from the British Library.
No part of this publication may be reproduced, stored in a retrieval system or transmitted in any form or by
any means, electronic, mechanical, photocopying, recording or otherwise, without the prior permission of
HarperCollins Publishers Ltd, 1 London Bridge Street, London SE1 9GF.

1 3 5 7 9 10 8 6 4 2

Hardback ISBN: 978-0-00-832961-7
Export Paperback ISBN: 978-0-00-832960-0

Copyright © 2019 by Dr. Seuss Enterprises, L.P.
All rights reserved

Adapted and original material in this book originally appeared in *One Fish Two Fish Red Fish Blue Fish*,
TM & © by Dr. Seuss Enterprises, L.P. 1960, 1988; *Green Eggs and Ham*, TM & © by Dr. Seuss Enterprises,
L.P. 1960, 1988, 2003; *McElligot's Pool*, TM & © by Dr. Seuss Enterprises, L.P. 1947, 1974; *Hop on Pop*,
TM & © by Dr. Seuss Enterprises, L.P. 1963, 1991; *How the Grinch Stole Christmas!* and *The Cat in the Hat*,
both TM & © by Dr. Seuss Enterprises, L.P. 1957, 1985; *Horton Hatches the Egg*, TM & © by
Dr. Seuss Enterprises, L.P. 1940, 1968; *Oh, The Thinks You Can Think!*, TM & © by Dr. Seuss Enterprises,
L.P. 1975, 2003; *The Sneetches and Other Stories*, TM & © by Dr. Seuss Enterprises, L.P. 1961, 1989;
Happy Birthday to You!, TM & © by Dr. Seuss Enterprises, L.P. 1959, 1982.

First published in hardback and paperback in the UK in 2019 by HarperCollins Children's Books, a division
of HarperCollins Publishers Ltd, 1 London Bridge Street, London SE1 9GF.

www.harpercollins.co.uk

Printed and bound in China

LOVE

from

Dr. Seuss™

HarperCollins *Children's Books*

One love,

Two love,

I love,

You love.

One Fish,
Two Fish,
Me Fish,
You Fish.

From there to here,
from here to there,
so much love
is everywhere!

I would **love** you
in the rain.
And in the **dark.**
And on a train.
And in a car.
And in a tree.
Because **you** are
the one for **me!**

I love you,
here or there.
I would love you
anywhere.

Oh, the sea is so full
of a number of fish.
If a fellow is patient,
he might get his wish.

He, Me,
He loves me!
She, Me,
She loves me!

I have a
thing
for you!

I meant
what I said
and I said what I meant...
I'll always be faithful
one hundred percent!

Love left
and love right
and love low
and love high.

Today I love you,
that is **truer** than **true**.
There is **no one** around
I love more
than **you**.